"*This little gem of a book was written by an expatriate Brit who has resided in Japan for several years, and whose love for that nation's culture, traditions, and people shines through in five short stories about Japanese senior citizens. Ashton's writing is spare and concise, analogous in style to Japanese calligraphy, haiku poetry, or ikebana – and it is precisely this elegant simplicity which gives his work such profound emotional power and quiet beauty.*"

"*This is a delightful and gentle collection of short stories based on the author's long residence in Japan and his personal knowledge of the ageing society there. As is well known, Japan is at the forefront of the societies confronting this problem, and we don't often get such well-written insights into how that feels and impacts on daily life. These tales are told with humour and sympathy, and may help to open a few eyes as to what living in Japan is really like for and among the silver generation.*"

"*I was pleased to find that the stories are refreshingly free of clichés. There are no stories of seniors confused by grandchildren with their smartphones, video games and teenage slang. Also, there are no stories of "international marriages", with stereotyped Japanese old codgers rolling out the old fears of inter-cultural misunderstandings and getting flustered by "foreigners" using chopsticks – I am SO TIRED of that kind of writing. Instead what we do have are characters that come across as real people, portrayed in a wistful and dryly humorous way, in a style that reminded this reviewer of Norwegian Wood'-era Murakami.*"

Tales of Old Japanese

Hugh Ashton

Published by j-views Publishing, 2018

ISBN-13: 978-1-912605-53-8

ISBN-10: 1-91-260553-8

j-views Publishing, 26 Lombard Street,
Lichfield, WS13 6DR

publish@j-views.biz

www.j-views.biz

www.HughAshtonBooks.com

TALES OF
OLD JAPANESE

DEDICATION

I would like to dedicate these stories to the following:

To Kiyoshi and Kikuno Nishio, my parents-in-law, sadly no longer with us, who provided a link to Japan's past. I felt very privileged to be living in your house which you loved so much. The little decorations between sections of these stories are the Nishio family *mon* or crest.

To all the people of Japan, and especially those of Tohoku who were hit by the triple disaster of March 11, 2011. Your courage and *gaman* served as an inspiration, not just to me, but to all those non-Japanese living in this country, and to the whole world.

To Inknbeans Press, and to the memory of Jo, who helped shape these stories into their final form.

To Nikki McBroom who has translated my words into images so skilfully.

And to my wife, Yoshiko, whose loving patience makes it possible for me to write these stories.

CONTENTS

PREFACE TO 2012 EDITION

These stories celebrate the histories, the lives, and the quirks of older people living in Japan, a country where I have spent the past twenty-four years. For those of you who know Japan as either an over-industrialised nation with smokestacks and pollution, inhabited by blue-suited white-shirted worker ants, or as a country of youth-oriented manga and anime cartoons where everyone dresses like a superhero, or even as a geisha and cherry blossom land, the stories in this book may come as something of a surprise.

Once you move out of Tokyo and you live in the suburbs, life becomes slower, and there is time to observe the people around you. As you get to know them, you realise that there is a wealth of history out there, and sometimes some painful memories are hidden behind the smiles. These stories are all based around the older people in my neighbourhood whom I have come to know. None of these, of course, is a recognisable portrait of any one individual, but they all have some basis in the characters and the places around me.

Keiko's House and *Haircuts* both reflect the events of the Pacific War (which we call the Second World War) and the effect it had on some Japanese people. Especially for those readers who live in North America, it may be hard to imagine the devastation caused by the fire-bombings of Japanese cities, and the heartbreak that was caused by this destruction. Some of the events in *Keiko's House* actually occurred, and some are pieced together from what I have learned from those who lived through those times. For those who served Japan abroad in the Imperial Army or Navy, the war brought its own memories, and some of these are imagined in *Haircuts*.

When Japanese people take up a hobby or an interest, they are typically whole-hearted and enthusiastic about it. Such enthusiasm bordering on obsession, in this case for photography, forms the basis for *Click*, and to a certain extent for *Mrs Sakamoto's Grouse*, though the latter also deals with affection and loss.

Lastly, a good old-fashioned ghost story to end the collection, based around an old house that used to stand near where we live now. *The Old House* actually existed, though as far as I know it was never haunted.

All these stories except *Click* had their first airing at a writers' group which met in Ben's Café in Takadanobaba (unhappily now defunct) run by Yoshiko Toyama, whenever there was a fifth Sunday in the month, and writers in English used to assemble and read their latest works to each other. *The Old House* was written for a Halloween which happened to be such a fifth Sunday.

Hugh Ashton
Kamakura, March 2012

TALES OF OLD JAPANESE

HUGH ASHTON

ILLUSTRATIONS BY

NIKKI McBROOM

J-VIEWS PUBLISHING, LICHFIELD, ENGLAND

KEIKO'S HOUSE

AUTHOR'S NOTE

When I originally wrote this, I deliberately wrote it without punctuation to mark off speech and thoughts, as I wanted to convey the kind of dream-state where the line between reality and imagination becomes blurred that is so easy to enter in the hot Japanese summer.

*T*here he was again. Sitting on the Matsuokas' garden wall by the roadside. Keiko had seen him hanging round the area for the past few weeks, but she still hadn't told anyone about him. He looked old, maybe eighty or so, about twenty years older than Keiko, but still fit. He must have been a tall man once, she guessed, but now age had bent him and he stooped awkwardly. One arm always seemed to be hanging stiffly by his side – she'd once noticed him fishing a packet of cigarettes out of the pocket of his scruffy stained blazer, extracting a cigarette and lighting it, all one-handed.

Why hadn't she told anyone about him? she asked herself. Well, it was stupid to be frightened of an old man like this, she told herself. If she told the police about him, they'd just laugh. What had he done, anyway? He was just there. Not doing anything. He didn't even seem to be particularly interested in her, just the house.

The house had been her parents' house. A handsome building, in traditional Japanese style, fitting the mood of this traditional area of the small town outside Yokohama, it had been built before the war by her father. Keiko had been born and grown up there. Well, she hadn't actually been born there, she had to admit. She'd been born in the worst part of the war, when the Americans were regularly sending the *B-san* bombers over Japanese cities, raining fire and destruction down on the wooden houses of the people below. Her mother, who had grown up in the northern island of Hokkaido, had travelled all the way back up there by train, through the length of wartime Japan, accompanied by her elder daughter, then three years old, to give birth to Keiko in the familiar surroundings of her own parents' home. It had been a particularly difficult birth, and she'd had to spend several months in hospital with Keiko, her new baby, before she was judged well enough to make the long and arduous journey back to her husband.

Some time later, she had returned to her husband's house, and Keiko had spent the rest of her life living in the house, first with her parents, then when her mother died, with her father, and lastly, when he had died a few years later, alone.

Her father had lived in the house like a turtle in its shell. It seemed more like a part of his own body than a building he inhabited.

He hated to leave it empty, never leaving it without making Keiko, or her mother, when she was alive, stay inside to guard it. Against what? she had asked him one day.

Burglars and fire, he replied.

That was absurd, she told herself, but didn't dare say this to him. In this quiet residential area, robbery was almost unknown. And fire? They'd stopped cooking on charcoal stoves soon after the war. The new gas cookers were so much safer.

He'd worried about so many things, she sighed to herself. They'd had a terrible battle about her being allowed her own key to the house, when she was fifty years old. He'd claimed she was not to be trusted, following an incident when she'd once left the front door unlocked at the age of twenty, thirty years before.

Children at elementary school get their own keys now, she'd told him.

And you've not got as much sense as an elementary school child, he'd answered angrily. She didn't get the key then, but did acquire one a few years later when he went into hospital with a minor heart attack.

Her sister, Fumiko, had moved out to get married at the age of twenty. Once married, she stayed well away from the house after her mother had died, preferring to live with her husband at the other end of Japan, in Kyushu. Once or twice a year she had come without her husband to stay at the house and look after their father for a week or so, and Keiko took this opportunity to go away with friends on short vacations to hot spring resorts.

Life had become much easier since her father had died of a second heart attack, but she had to admit that she missed his presence around the house. More than that, she missed her mother, who'd been her friend as much as her mother. As she talked to the neighbours, Keiko came to realise that her mother seemed to have been a friend to the whole neighbourhood. Old Mrs Suzuki, who lived next door, still talked wistfully of the cucumber pickles that Keiko's mother used to make. Keiko had long since given away the rice bran mixture that her mother had used, but still felt guilty that she wasn't still turning over the cucumbers in their nest of bran and salt every morning and replacing the finished pickles with fresh cucumbers. Now she bought her pickles from the supermarket. They didn't taste so good, but they were a lot easier to deal with, especially since she only had to consider herself now. It didn't stop the house feeling lonely, though.

She put down her shopping bag and felt in her purse for her keys. She unlocked the door, and bent down to pick up her shopping. As she did so, she felt the man's eyes on her. Or rather, as she looked more closely, they weren't on her, but were looking past her, through the open door into the house.

Why are you doing this? What are you looking at? she wanted to shout. This is my house! But she didn't.

Instead she picked up her bag and marched straight through the open door. She peeked out just before shutting the door and bolting it. He was still there.

What a day! The heat was almost unbearable inside the house with the windows closed. She opened the windows and then went to the refrigerator to pour herself a glass of *mugi-cha* – barley tea, which she sipped with pleasure. As she drank it, it occurred to her that it would be an act of kindness to take a drink out to the old man sitting out there. He looked old and tired, and he was probably thirsty. She reached into the back of the cupboard and got out one of the old glasses that she hadn't used since her mother had died. Somehow it seemed appropriate to be using one of these old-fashioned glasses for the old man.

Glass of cold barley tea in hand, she approached the old man, whose gaze now seemed to be fixed on her kitchen window. He didn't seem to notice her until she asked him if he would like something to drink.

His thanks were polite, and given in a deep voice that seemed to come from someone other than the frail old man in front of her. He gravely took the glass from her and slowly drank the cold brown liquid as she watched. When he had finished, he turned the empty glass in his hands, studying it carefully as if he'd never seen a glass before.

It's old, isn't it? he asked with a toothless smile. About as old as I am, I would guess.

I don't know, she replied. Maybe. She suddenly realised that these glasses had always been a part of her life. She couldn't remember a time when they hadn't been there.

Your name is Inoue? he asked suddenly.

Keiko gave a little start of surprise and then told herself

that it was easy for him to find out these things. After all, her family name was written on a sign by the front door. She said nothing, but nodded.

Are there still five of these glasses? was his next strange question. One of them with a small crack just here? as he pointed to a spot at the base of the glass.

Four, she replied without thinking. One broke more than ten years ago. Not the one with the crack. Amazingly, she remembered the day that the glass had broken. Her mother had been heartbroken over the loss and had actually wept tears as she swept up the fragments. It was because of this association that Keiko had decided not to use the glasses for herself as everyday utensils.

Keiko was overcome with curiosity. How did he come to know about the contents of her crockery cupboard?

Well, nothing lasts forever, I suppose, he replied, as she was pondering the mystery. He seemed to be wondering what to say next.

Without knowing why she was doing it, Keiko found herself inviting him inside. You must be hot, she said to him, and took the glass from his hand. Please come inside and relax a little.

He bowed his thanks and followed her into the porch, taking off his shoes and arranging them neatly as he stepped up into the hallway.

Shyly, he asked if he could use her toilet.

Of course, she replied. It's over there.

Oh, I know where it is, was his astonishing reply. He made his way straight to the toilet with no hesitation. She waited for him to come out after washing his hands, and showed him into the living room.

As he stepped into the room, his attention was caught by the *butsudan* with its photos of Keiko's mother and father. He let out an exclamation, and instantly asked her permission to pay his respects.

Kneeling on the cushion, he lit a candle and one of the incense sticks and knelt silently, his head bowed, for several minutes. His actions seemed like more than mere polite ritual.

She had another glass of barley tea ready for him when he finally arose.

Excuse me, he said to her after he had settled himself on the tatami. You are Fumiko?

No, Fumiko is my older sister. I am Keiko.

Oh, he said, and his face seemed to brighten. He smiled. I have something for you.

Keiko was not sure if she was in the presence of a madman or not. Without really thinking what she was doing, she shrank away from this strange man.

Please, he said. You mustn't be frightened. He reached inside his jacket and pulled something out of the pocket there. Now Keiko noticed that his other arm was missing below the elbow. The jacket's sleeve swung empty from halfway down. He handed her the small purple silk-wrapped package that he had been carrying in his jacket.

Please, open it, he invited.

Unknotting the neatly tied silk, Keiko pulled out a plain gold ring.

Please, look inside the ring.

Keiko adjusted her glasses and held the ring up to the light, peering at her parents' initials in English letters, and a date that she recognised as their wedding date.

Who are you, and what are you doing with this? she asked him, suddenly angry. What was this stranger doing to her and how was he linked with her family? she asked herself. She had to bite her lip hard to keep herself from bursting into a flood of emotional tears.

Keiko, you don't know me. You've never met me, but I'm your oldest friend, he replied. Before you were born, I was living in this house. I was a young naval officer serving at the base near here, and I was billeted on your family. Your mother especially was very kind to me. Like a wonderful big sister. Your father, too. When I heard that my parents had been killed in an air raid on Tokyo, she held my hand, and she and your father talked to me and comforted me all night as I wept. I can never forget that night. We were sitting just there, where you are sitting now.

Keiko instinctively moved away from the spot he indicated.

I went back to Tokyo. The only thing left of their house was a box that contained those drinking glasses. One of the set of six was missing, and another was cracked, but I presented the box to your mother and father. It was all I could do at the time.

Keiko felt a lump rising in her throat.

But the ring? she asked. How did you come by that?

When your mother donated her jewellery to the war effort she gave everything, even her wedding ring. A lot of women didn't do that, but your mother did. I told your parents that I would take the jewellery straight to the navy base so that it wouldn't get stolen or lost. And that's what I did. Except for the ring. I was planning to give it back to them.

Why didn't you? Keiko asked him, touched by the story.

Your mother was pregnant with you. I knew that she wanted to get back to her parents where it would be safer for her to give birth to you, so I stole a blank form and forged an official pass for her to go up to Hokkaido. I was meaning to give her the ring back when she returned, but she spent longer than anyone expected, and my commanding officer found out what I'd done, so they shipped me overseas as a punishment. And then this happened, pointing to his half-empty sleeve.

Keiko wiped the tears from her eyes.

I've never dared come back here. I was frightened that this house I loved so much would be a hole in the ground, or there would be some horrible new apartment building here. I wasn't expecting to find any of the family who looked after me so well. And certainly not you.

There was a silence. Keiko closed her eyes and sat very still for a long time. There were some faint rustlings and noises, and then the sound of the front door opening and closing. Keiko's eyes snapped open. The old man was gone. The glass that he had been drinking from and the purple cloth that he'd pulled from his pocket were still on the table. And her hand still gripped the gold ring. She got to her feet and went to the front door. She opened it. No-one to be seen.

Ojī-san! Ojiī-san! Old man! she called, running to the road and looking around. No-one. Only a bicycle with a young girl on it.

Her hand still clutched the ring as she went back to the house. But now there was another spirit in the house – the spirit of the stranger whose actions had helped her come into the world. Somehow the house wasn't so lonely any more.

HAIRCUTS

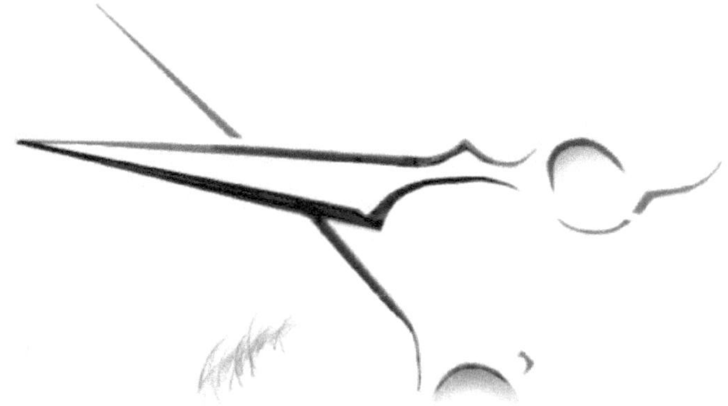

Mr Kato felt he was being cheated by his barber, Mr Uchiyama, who had been cutting his hair for the past forty years. At the age of ninety-two, Mr Kato had lost most of his hair, but he was still charged the same for his haircuts as if he had been a young man, though the operation now took a fraction of the time that it had done in the past. As a rather sprightly older man who still took some pride in his appearance, Mr Kato had his hair cut at least once a month and, while he was neither a mean nor a poor man, felt that Mr Uchiyama was lining his pockets at his (Mr Kato's) expense. As he returned from a haircut one day, his neighbour, Mrs Watanabe, called out to him.

"You look very smart." She was leaving her house to go shopping.

Mr Kato grunted, but it was a polite grunt. "Thank you," he acknowledged.

"But you don't look very happy." Mrs Watanabe felt she had the right to make such personal remarks. Before Mr Kato's wife had died from throat cancer, thirty years before, Mrs Watanabe had been her best friend, and still looked on Mr Kato, some twenty years her senior, as a sort of uncle.

"I'm not happy, really," admitted Mr Kato. "Nothing serious. In fact, it's really rather silly, but I really don't think I should be spending this sort of money on my haircuts. I mean," and he lifted his hat to demonstrate, "I really don't have that much hair to cut."

"Then you should do what Mr Watanabe does," said Mrs Watanabe, firmly. "Get your hair cut at one of those new places. They just cut your hair, and don't shave you, but it takes only ten minutes or so, and it's not expensive at only a thousand yen, and you hardly have to wait."

"Is there one of those near here?" asked Mr Kato. This sounded like a good idea. Despite his loyalty of the past decades, he'd show Mr Uchiyama that he didn't really need him.

"There's one just outside the next station along the line. Go out of the west exit and turn left."

"I'll remember that. Thank you, Mrs Watanabe."

About two weeks later, Mr Kato felt the need to have his hair cut again, but instead of making his way to Uchiyama's place down the road, he caught the train from his suburb to the centre of town. As Mrs Watanabe had told him, there was a shop, with a bold blue and white sign, advertising ten-minute haircuts for a thousand yen. What did he have to lose? he asked himself, and further fortified himself for the slight ordeal of having his hair cut by a stranger for the first time in over four decades by promising himself a sushi meal bought with the savings he would make on this.

As he entered the shop, he saw there were four chairs, all occupied, with young men cutting customers' hair, and the customers were women and children as well as men. Then he looked a little closer, and noticed that some of the barbers were girls. He supposed that the men would cut men's hair, and the girls would take care of the women and children.

There was a row of seats, and he took his place at the end of the row. There were four people in the line ahead of him; two men and a mother and a small boy. He watched the soap opera showing on television as he waited, and the chairs emptied and the line moved up one by one as the barbers finished attending to their customers. It certainly seemed quicker than Mr Uchiyama's place, where he could sometimes spend a whole afternoon waiting to be attended to. Now he was at the front of the line, and he heard a girl's voice calling for the next customer. Was he going to have his hair cut by a girl, then? He stood up and walked over to the empty chair. She held out her hand to him.

"Card, please."

He looked blank, and she smiled at him. "Is this your first time here?" He nodded, feeling a little foolish, and she led him to the door of the shop. There was a machine there with a notice on it telling him to buy a card before he started to wait in line to have his hair cut.

"Just put a thousand yen in here," she told him.

His fingers, stiffened by age, had problems unfolding the banknote and inserting it into the slot.

"May I?" she asked, taking the note and putting it into the slot. "Sometimes the machine doesn't work properly." The machine took the money and spat out a card. "See the card?" She pressed it into his hand.

He examined the small card, which told him that he was entitled to a haircut. He presented it to the girl, and allowed himself to be led to one of the chairs.

"How shall I cut it?" she asked him.

This was a bit of a problem. He hadn't been asked this question in more than forty years.

"Just do it the way you think best," he said, a little nervously. "Just don't do it too modern."

She laughed, and he felt happy inside. It seemed like it had been a long time since a girl had laughed at something he said. Still, he felt a bit nervous as she plugged in the clippers and picked up a comb. Her hand, as she held his head and guided the clippers up the back of his neck, felt soft and capable, not like Mr Uchiyama's hands, which were almost as gnarled and hard as Mr Kato's own.

"Do you live near here?" she asked him. He was pleased that his hearing was still good enough to understand what she was saying, even over the noise of the clippers.

"Just one station down the line," he told her.

"Oh, that's a nice area. Sometimes I take my dog for a walk there."

"What sort of dog is he?" he asked her.

"Mimi's a she, actually. She's a corgi. Like the dogs Queen Elizabeth of England has. Do you have a dog?"

"No." His dog had died a few years after his wife had died, and he hadn't wanted another, but he didn't tell her that.

"Sometimes I go to that coffee shop just near the temple there," she rattled on. "They make a really nice cappuccino and they make really delicious cookies. It's more like a café bakery than a traditional coffee shop."

Mr Kato, who had once visited Italy, and remembered the coffee there with pleasure, told her that he hadn't been, and asked her for the name of the place.

"It's got an English name, 'Stone Bridge'," she told him. "In English. The owner is called Mr Ishibashi."

"That's a good name for the shop, then," he smiled.

"Why?" she asked. The clippers moved around one ear, then the other.

"Because that's what Ishibashi means in English. Stone Bridge."

The clippers stopped buzzing, and she picked up a pair of scissors. "How clever of you to speak English so well."

He waved a self-deprecatory hand under the sheet covering his lap. "Just a little. One of my sons married an American and lives in California now."

"Do you go there at all?" Snip, snip.

"I'm too old now," he smiled. "But I went there several times when I was younger."

"You're not too old," she protested.

"Guess?" he invited.

"Oh, I don't know. Seventy-five?" She put away the thinning scissors and reached for a mirror to hold behind his head.

He shook his head.

"Don't you like it? Sorry."

"No, it's fine," he replied. "I'm a bit older than seventy-five, though."

"Over eighty?" He nodded. "Over eighty-five?" Another nod. "You're going to have to tell me."

"Ninety-two," he said, with more than a touch of pride.

"Well, I'd never have guessed. And you came here on your own?"

"Of course," he said. "I live on my own. Make my own breakfast. They deliver my evening meals, and sometimes one of the day helpers comes in to give me my lunch."

"And what are you going to do for lunch after this? Go home? It will be time after I've finished here."

"I'm going to the *kaiten sushi* place where the plates come round on the conveyor belt."

"Well, I *am* impressed." She brushed the back of his neck and took off the sheet, handing him a warm wet towel to wipe his face. He wiped, and handed the cloth back to her.

"Excuse me, do you mind? You have something in the corner of your eye." She gently cleaned the sleep from his eyes with the corner of the towel, holding his chin in her hand as if he were a child. He felt comforted by the feeling.

"There you are, all gone."

"Thank you." He stood up.

"Don't forget your glasses," handing them to him.

"You're very kind," he told her. "Will you cut my hair next time?"

"Of course I'd like to," she smiled. "If I'm here and you're the next in line. But we can't really choose our customers here."

"I see." He was a bit disappointed. Having only just made the change of hairdresser, he was rather hoping that he could develop a new sense of permanence. Anyway, he liked this girl. She seemed sensible, and he noticed that she was rather pretty. Even at ninety-two, these things matter, he told himself. "Never mind. See you next time. Thank you very much."

"Thank you," she replied, as he left the shop.

About a week after he had had his hair cut, Mr Kato went out to post a letter. He decided to return to his house a different way from the one by which he had set out, as he needed to buy some milk and some eggs. As he turned the corner towards the supermarket, he noticed the name of the café near the temple. "Stone Bridge" – where had he heard that name before? Oh yes, when he was having his hair cut. He stood still as he tried to remember what the conversation had been about. Oh yes, the name of the shop and the name of the owner, translated into English. He smiled at the memory as a small brown dog rushed towards him, and ran against his legs, nearly knocking him over.

"Oh, so sorry. Are you all right?" asked the young lady on the other end of the dog's leash. "Oh!" She sounded surprised.

He looked up from the dog, and recognized the face. "Oh, it's you!" His wrinkled face broke into a wide smile, and a sudden impulse hit him as he remembered the conversation he'd had with her while he was having his hair cut. "Let's have coffee together."

Her smile was just as wonderful as he remembered and he was glad he'd made the suggestion. "I was just going to have a cup of coffee there. Yes, let's have our coffee together."

"What about..?" he pointed to the dog.

"Oh, Mimi-chan can come in. Mr Ishibashi's really good about letting people's pets come in with them."

Despite the fact that he'd lived near the coffee shop since it had opened, he had never been inside it, or even spoken to Mr Ishibashi, who lived only about a hundred meters away from him. Curious.

He opened the door and held it for her. "After you."

"Oh, you must be a real gentleman." He felt himself blushing as she and her dog went into the café.

As she'd said, the owner of the coffee shop seemed to look after his customers and their dogs. As Mr Kato's new friend chose a table, he bustled up with a basket with a cushion inside, into which she lifted the dog. The table was by the window, and had two chairs. She'd pulled one out for him when he reached the table.

"Thank you," he said, sitting down. "I remember you

said the cappuccino here is good. Is that what you're going to drink?"

"Yes. Are you going to have some cookies?"

"I'm not a great fan of sweet things usually."

"These are really good, though. They're homemade. I know what, I'll give you a piece of my cookie, and if you don't like it, then nothing's been wasted, has it?"

It sounded rather daring to Mr Kato, sharing a girl's food like this. He realised that he didn't even know her name. He asked.

"Yoko. What's yours?"

"Kato."

"That's your family name. What's your other name?"

"Well, I really don't think it's suitable for you to use that name to me, is it?" As an older Japanese man, Mr Kato was very much a traditionalist. It was all very well for him to call this young woman by her given name, and to add the affectionate *-chan* at the end if he wanted, but it really wasn't her place to start calling him 'Hideki'. She smiled at him, but said nothing. The coffee maker hissed and bubbled in the background, and the aroma of freshly brewed coffee filled the air.

The coffees arrived, together with a cookie on a plate for Yoko. She carefully broke off a small piece and put it on the saucer beside his cup.

"It's cinnamon and almond," she told him.

"That sounds interesting," he said. "I don't think I've ever tried that sort of cookie before."

He put a spoonful of sugar into his cup, and stirred carefully, trying not to disturb the foam. He took a sip of the coffee, and picked up the piece of cookie.

"Mmmm, that's delicious," he said, as he chewed slowly.

It seemed as though it had been a long time since he'd tasted anything like it.

"Shall I order you a whole one for yourself?"

"Yes please." His cookie soon arrived, and he scrupulously broke off a piece of about the size Yoko had given to him, and passed it back to her.

"Oh, please don't worry about that," she said, but he insisted.

As he reached over to put the cookie fragment on her plate, he noticed someone looking through the window. He looked more carefully, and saw it was Mrs Watanabe, his neighbour. She looked surprised. Almost shocked. Well, what was wrong with his having a cup of coffee? He deposited the piece of cookie on Yoko-chan's plate and waved. Yoko followed his glance to the definitely shocked Mrs Watanabe, who didn't return the wave, but turned away hurriedly and bustled off.

"A friend of yours?" asked Yoko.

"Yes. My neighbour. I think she's a bit surprised by what she just saw." He started to laugh quietly. "She's probably going to tell the whole neighbourhood now about my new girlfriend."

"Oh dear, I am sorry. I hope this won't cause problems with your wife." Mr Kato stopped laughing. "Oh dear," she repeated as she watched his face. "I forgot that you live alone. I am sorry."

"It was a long time ago. I should have got used to it. Don't worry." He examined the fingers of Yoko's left hand. "You're not married?"

"I was. Now I'm not. A good thing, really."

The background music came to an end and an awkward silence seemed to descend on the place, broken only by Mimi's snuffling in her basket.

"Well, let's cheer up," said Mr Kato. "Tell me something about yourself."

"Nothing to tell, really. I was born near here. Never done anything much. But you must have done an awful lot in your time. For example," she hesitated a little, "you must have lived through the war?"

It was an invitation to talk, and Mr Kato found himself talking about his time in the war, and the time he had spent in Malaya and Singapore when he was a cook for the Imperial Japanese Army. "I'm boring you," he said, after a while. "Sorry. It seems to do me good to talk about these things to someone who's not been bored by them before."

"But it's not boring, honestly. And it explains how you can look after yourself. My father can't even make a piece of toast or a cup of tea for himself. I think you're wonderful."

Mr Kato felt something inside that he hadn't felt for a long time. Shyness, embarrassment and sheer pleasure at being alive all combined to make him smile. "Thank you," was all he could manage.

"Oh, I mean it. Now, I said I'm not bored and I really mean that, but," looking at her watch, "I really must be going." She stood up and walked to the cash register, Mimi-chan leaving her basket and following her. Mr Kato stood up and followed her, feeling for his wallet.

"Don't worry," she said. "I've paid for you. It's the least I can do to apologise for my stupidity."

"But..." He pulled a thousand-yen note from his wallet, and tried to thrust it on her, but she refused. "Please," she said. "You can pay next time."

The idea that she was even talking about a next time

sent a thrill of pleasure down Mr Kato's spine. "All right then," he agreed. "When will that be?"

"Tuesday's my day off, so next Tuesday. I'll see you here at eleven o'clock?"

"Yes. Thank you for the coffee. Take care of yourself."

They waved goodbye to each other outside the shop. Mimi turned her head and barked a farewell.

After he had gone to the supermarket and bought his milk and eggs (he was quite proud of himself for having remembered them after the excitement of the morning), Mr Kato would have skipped back home if his back had allowed it. He certainly felt lighter on his feet than usual, and his legs, which usually pained him after walking more than a few hundred metres, felt as though they were twenty or thirty years younger. He wasn't conscious of walking fast, but he realised that he must have been going faster than usual, as he felt himself a little out of breath as he turned the corner to the short rise leading to his house.

Mrs Watanabe was standing outside her front door. She appeared to be doing something to the hydrangea bush there, but it seemed to Mr Kato that she had been waiting for him, and had only just snatched up the secateurs in order to have an excuse to be there.

"Well!" she said to him, putting her hands on her hips, as he drew alongside her house.

There wasn't really any answer that Mr Kato could give to that, so he stopped, and put his head on one side.

"Holding hands with that young woman! And at your age! Really!" Mrs Watanabe seemed to be quite upset.

"I wasn't holding hands," he protested. He didn't see why he had to justify himself to Mrs Watanabe, but she seemed to expect some sort of answer.

"I saw you," she retorted. "In full view of everyone." Now he remembered that as he had held the cookie fragment over her plate, she had tried to push his hand and the cookie away, protesting that he didn't need to worry about returning a small piece of cookie. "What do you think the neighbours will think?"

"I know what one of them thinks already," he replied. "And I know what the others will think if that neighbour goes round spreading gossip about me." His voice came out a little sharper than he had intended.

To his surprise and horror, Mrs Watanabe started to cry. "I really didn't mean that," she sniffled. "I was just so shocked after knowing you so long. I don't know..." She tailed off.

"Please accept my apologies." By now Mr Kato was hopelessly embarrassed again. "Never mind me, what will people think of you if they see you crying like this?"

"You're right. I must pull myself together." She wiped her eyes, and looked at Mr Kato. "Who is she, anyway?"

"She works at the barber's. The one you suggested I went to. The one who cuts your hair for a thousand yen."

"Oh?"

"She started talking to me as she cut my hair last week and I ran into her by accident today. She suggested that we have a cup of coffee together."

"I see." Mrs Watanabe seemed lost in thought. "She's quite pretty, isn't she? How old do you think she is?"

The question took Mr Kato a little by surprise. "I hadn't really thought about it. She's been married, though."

"But she isn't married now?" Mrs Watanabe pounced. "You take care, now." She seemed to have changed from being shocked to sounding concerned, but there was still an edge there. "These young girls with older men..." Her voice trailed off.

Mr Kato was somewhat taken aback. He was glad, at least, that Mrs Watanabe hadn't said 'old men', just 'older men'. "I'm not sure that I really understand what you're saying, but please don't worry, anyway. All that happened is that she talked to me last week when she cut my hair, and then we met by accident this morning."

"Hmph." Mrs Watanabe sniffed. "Well, I must get back to my gardening." Mr Kato noticed that there were no flowers or leaves on the ground, confirming his suspicion that the hydrangea pruning had been simply an excuse to wait outside for him to turn up.

On the next Tuesday, Mr Kato took a little more time shaving than usual, examining his face carefully in the mirror, and dressed himself with special care, picking out one of his better shirts, and making sure that he had no spots or stains on his trousers.

Should he wear a tie? he asked himself, but after his fingers clumsily failed to tie the knot after several attempts, he decided not to bother. Why was he doing this? he asked himself. Was it because this girl was the daughter he'd always secretly wished he and his wife had had, instead of their two sons? He decided that he wasn't being honest with himself. He didn't really want to put into words what he felt, but it reminded him of his younger days. Much younger days.

At five to eleven, he was sitting in Stone Bridge, his hands, on top of the table, fidgeting in an unfamiliar way. He looked at them, as if for the first time. Maybe they weren't the world's most beautiful hands, but they didn't look old. At least, not that old. Not ninety-two years old, anyway.

He saw Mimi first, straining at her leash. And then Yoko, following, dressed in a pair of clean jeans and a pale yellow T-shirt. As she entered, he stood up clumsily, and smiled. She smiled back, in just the way that he remembered her smiling.

"Let's sit down," she smiled. "Cappuccino for you today?" He nodded. "Now I know that you liked the cinnamon and almond cookie the other day, but there's another one they do here that's one of my favourites. Let me order for you and you can guess what it is."

"That sounds fine." He sat back contented as Yoko talked to Mr Ishibashi to order the coffee. To his horror, he realized that Mrs Watanabe was frowning through the window at him. "Go away," he mouthed, and made a flapping motion with his hand. Yoko saw him, and turned to the window.

"Oh it's her," she said. "Your neighbour. Please wait a minute." She stood up, and went out of the shop. Mr Kato saw her approach Mrs Watanabe and say something to her, and started what looked like an animated conversation. Amazingly, after a few moments Mrs Watanabe seemed to be smiling as she shook her head and turned away. Yoko came back in and sat down. She, too, was smiling.

"What did you say?" asked Mr Kato.

"I introduced myself and asked her if she wanted to join us. I thought from what you said last time, and the way she was looking just now that she rather disapproved of me, so I thought it was a good idea for me to talk to her and let her know I am harmless." She smiled. "I think I persuaded her. Don't worry about her."

The coffees and cookies arrived. "Now, what is this?" asked Yoko, passing one of the cookie plates to him.

He took a nibble of his cookie and chewed thoughtfully. "Hmmm… There's some vanilla in here. And something else. Something nutty-tasting, but I can't put a name to it. Yes I can. It's coconut."

"*Pin-pon*," she sang out, echoing the standard 'correct' answer on TV game shows. "You're right about the vanilla. And the coconut. How very clever of you." He glowed.

"The coconut reminds me of Malaya and Singapore," he said. "When I was there, we seemed to eat a lot of coconut." The taste of the coconut brought a memory of drinking coconut juice with a Chinese girl one evening swimming up into his memory. She'd been beautiful and kind, he remembered, even though their only common language had been a pidgin Malay. He'd only met her three times – each meeting was etched on his memory – and then one day he'd gone to her house and there was no-one there. A neighbour had shouted from the window that the girl and her family had been arrested by the *Kempetai* – the Imperial Army's political police. He'd never had the courage to investigate further. Even now, he felt a sense of loss that forty years of contented marriage had failed to eliminate. And now he had started to remember, he realized that Yoko reminded him in several ways of Chen Shueng Man. He still remembered her name, after all these years. Strange...

"Are you all right?" Yoko broke into his thoughts.

"What? Oh, yes. Thank you." He sniffed and realized that he'd started to weep silently without being aware of it. How long had he been in his daydreams of the past? He pulled out a handkerchief.

"No, let me do that," she said. As she had done previously in the barber's, she wiped his eyes for him.

"Were you thinking of your wife?" she asked sympathetically.

"Yes," he lied. "Sorry." He covered his embarrassment by picking up his cappuccino and taking a sip. As he put the cup down, she started laughing.

"I'm sorry," she said. "I shouldn't laugh, but you have some milk foam on the end of your nose. Please, allow me," and once again, she dabbed his face with her handkerchief. "I'm sorry," she repeated. "But it did look rather funny." She lowered her face into her cup, and when she emerged, her nose had a white dot on it. "You see?"

Mr Kato started to laugh. "Of course you laughed at me. It does look funny, I agree." She wiped the milk from her nose.

"It does, doesn't it? You know, you remind me of..." She paused. Mr Kato was sure she was going to say 'my grandfather' or some other elderly relative, but he was surprised when she finished the sentence with "...a boy I used to know in elementary school. He always had a dirty nose."

"I don't know whether that's a compliment or not," he said. But he was smiling.

"Oh, definitely a compliment. He was my best friend."

"Thank you," he said, and took another bite of coconut cookie. There was a pause of several minutes while they drank their coffees and ate their cookies. Mimi lapped at the bowl of water that had been brought for her and placed by her basket.

"I feel very comfortable sitting here with you," he said, breaking the silence.

"What a nice thing to say. Yes, I feel the same." She looked at her watch. "I hope you don't think I'm being rude or anything, but I have to be off soon. Usually this is my day off, but one of the other people at the barber's has to go to the dentist this afternoon, so I have to cover for her. It's not that I'm bored or anything – please don't think that."

"Do you want to go now?"

"Oh, no. Not just yet. But I must keep an eye on the time. Please tell me a bit more about what it was like in Singapore when you were there. I went there on holiday a few years ago, but I'm sure it was completely different then."

"I'm sure it was." He smiled. "But you don't want to hear an old man's stories. Would you mind if we talked about Mimi instead? How old is she?"

"If you prefer." She looked a little disappointed. "She was a little puppy when we – I got her." He noticed the correction, but didn't comment. "And that was about four or five years ago. When she was a puppy, she ate everything – even a pair of my shoes once. At least I think she must have done – they just disappeared one day, and she couldn't have taken them outside."

He laughed. "It doesn't seem to have affected her too badly." Indeed, Mimi did seem to be rather sleek and prosperous. They chatted some more about dogs in general, and Mimi in particular, and she looked at her watch again.

"This is terribly rude of me, but I must go. Oh, you haven't finished your cookie. Don't you like it?"

"Oh, I do like it but actually, I was wondering if Mr Ishibashi would wrap up this half for me and let me take it home for my dessert this evening."

"I'll ask him." She got up and talked to the café's owner.

"No problem," said Mr Ishibashi, picking up the half-cookie with tongs, and putting it into a bag with the café's name on it.

"Thank you," replied Mr Kato. "And here's the money to pay for both of us. No, no," as Yoko started to protest. "We agreed last time that I'd be doing the paying, remember?"

As they left the shop, Mr Kato suddenly said to Yoko, "Please wait a moment," and he dodged into the shop next door.

He came out of the flower shop a couple of minutes later with a small bouquet, which he presented to Yoko.

"I know it's not much," he said, handing the bunch of anemones to her, "but I just wanted to thank you for a lovely morning, and for talking to Mrs Watanabe, and... everything."

"Oh, thank you," she said. "You really shouldn't, but how lovely, and how kind of you." She lowered her nose into the bouquet and sniffed. "Oh, they're wonderful. Smell them." And she extended the bouquet towards him. Their faces were very close as he sniffed one side of the bouquet and she inhaled the flowers' scent on the other side.

"Oh yes. I didn't really notice when I bought them. You're right. Yes. Wonderful."

Without warning, she pecked him on the cheek. "You are so sweet." He was shocked, but thrilled at the same time. "Here " she added, removing an anemone from the bunch. "For you." And she planted it in his buttonhole. "Now I really must go."

She waved goodbye, Mimi in her wake.

Mr Kato watched her go out of sight round the corner, and then turned towards home, his hand full of a bag of cookie, and his heart full of conflicting emotions.

The next morning, Mrs Watanabe realised that she hadn't seen Mr Kato since she'd spied him through the café window the previous day. Come to that, there'd been no lights on in the house the previous evening. She noticed these things about her neighbours.

She marched up to Mr Kato's door and rang the bell. There was no answer. Strange. Perhaps he was round the back, in the garden? She couldn't see through the fence, but maybe he'd hear the telephone if she called him. His hearing was still excellent, she knew.

She pulled out her mobile phone and called the number. No answer. Strange. Now she was starting to get a little concerned. She rang again, and shouted through the half-open kitchen window. And that was strange, too. Usually he closed all the windows when he went to bed, and the window was open last evening.

This was getting worrying. Once again she pulled out her mobile phone, but this time she called the emergency services. Once the fire engine arrived a few minutes later, the fireman in charge asked her what this was all about, and she told him.

He sucked his teeth. "If the doors are locked, we'll have to break them down. Will you take the responsibility for this?" he asked.

"I suppose so. But couldn't you get through that window?" she suggested.

"That's an idea," he agreed. One of the fireman fetched a short ladder and wriggled through the gap. A few minutes later, there was a shout from inside.

"Call an ambulance."

"Oh dear," said Mrs Watanabe. "I hope he's all right." She shouted to the fireman inside the house. "Can you please open the door to let me in? Maybe I can help?"

The front door opened a minute later. "I don't think you should touch anything, though," the fireman told Mrs Watanabe as she kicked off her shoes.

"Is he all right?" she replied.

He shook his head.

"He's…?"

"Almost certainly, I'm afraid. He's cold. It probably happened yesterday."

She started to cry silently as he led the way to the kitchen. Mr Kato was seated at the table, dressed the way she'd seen him in the café, with a flower in his buttonhole. On the table in front of him were two cakes on two pieces of paper. One cake looked like a half-eaten cookie, on a napkin saying "Stone Bridge" - the name of the café where she'd seen him yesterday. The other seemed Chinese, somehow. She'd never seen anything quite like it. And the paper it rested on was a crumpled piece of yellowing newspaper, printed in Chinese. She looked closely. The date was 1942. There were a few words in

English in the middle of the Chinese. One, she read, was "Singapore".

Wiping away her tears, she looked at Mr Kato's face. He seemed at peace with himself. Wherever he'd gone, it seemed that he'd been happy to go there.

The ambulance siren sounded, and two paramedics came into the room, carrying a stretcher.

"What do you think happened?" the fireman asked them.

"How old was he, do you know?" the ambulance man asked Mrs Watanabe.

"Ninety-two," she answered. "And really *genki* – lively, healthy."

"At that age, the most likely thing is heart failure, I'm afraid."

Mrs Watanabe didn't answer. She didn't think that Mr Kato's ninety-two year-old heart had failed. After talking to the girl yesterday and looking at Mr Kato's face, she was convinced that his heart had sprung to life again for the first time in decades, and Mr Kato had died of happiness.

CLICK

No-one could ever remember seeing Mrs Terada without her camera. Whether she was shopping in the supermarket, out walking in the Tokyo suburb where she lived, or visiting friends, the camera was always there, either peeking out of her purse, or hanging round her neck. It wasn't one of the newer digital cameras, either. It was small, true, but it was a film camera, and the styling was definitely not modern.

"Can you still buy film for it?" incredulous friends asked her.

"Oh yes," she replied. "Of course, it's not as easy to find as it was, but you can still buy it in lots of places, and I can always get it."

"And what about developing and printing?"

"I take my films to the same shop I've used for twenty years. Mr Kawakami tells me that he's never going to give up developing and printing film. And he sells it, too. That's where I get the film for it. I'm not his only customer, you know."

The questioners would scratch their heads, puzzled by this stubborn middle-aged lady who seemed determined to live in the past.

"But isn't it terribly expensive?" they would ask. "I mean, digital pictures are so much cheaper."

"Not the way I take pictures," Mrs Terada explained. "I only take one picture each day."

"Only one each day?"

*I*t was true. Mrs Terada only took one photograph each day. She carried her camera around all the time in search of the perfect photo. Sometimes the moment came early in the day, sometimes she had to wait until the evening before the right picture presented itself to her. Then, taking her time, she carefully adjusted the settings of the camera to interpret the scene. Since the camera was an older model, lacking some of the automated features of more modern cameras, this could take a few minutes before she was satisfied. Finally, letting out her breath and bracing herself firmly to avoid shaking the camera, she squeezed the shutter release. After the click of the mechanism, she always stood still for a few seconds, seemingly imprinting the image firmly into her memory as she continued to gaze through the viewfinder. Even if she took her daily picture early in the morning, she still carried her camera round with her for the rest of the day. "So I never forget to carry it," she explained, a little enigmatically. Even when she'd gone into hospital for a minor operation, the camera went there with her. One of her favourite pictures was a group portrait of the nurses who'd cared for her, framed by the flowers that her friends had brought, taken from her hospital bed.

She bought her film in 24-exposure rolls. Every third Monday, she changed the roll, leaving three frames unexposed. Rain or shine, she then made her way to Mr Kawakami's shop, dropping the film in there for developing and printing, and buying another roll to be used in three weeks' time. On the Friday, she went to Mr Kawakami again, this time to pick up the prints of the film she had dropped in earlier in the week.

Of course, every shot was perfectly exposed. There was never any reason to throw away any of the prints.

They went into an album. Three postcard-sized prints to a page, with sixty pages in each album. That made one hundred and eighty pictures in an album, and Mrs Terada always added two or three to the inside back cover to turn each album into a record of exactly six months of her life. A little note accompanied each picture. When. Where. What. And why she had taken that particular picture. Two albums every year. Forty albums.

One of Mrs Terada's pleasures was looking over her memories, especially with friends. She'd pick one of the albums, seemingly at random, from off the shelf where they stood in chronological order.

"Wasn't he handsome in those days?" she'd ask, pointing to a picture of her late husband. Not that her pictures could be classed as family snapshots by any manner of means. Each picture of Mr Terada was of a quality that could be exhibited in a gallery. Composition, framing, focus, and the ability to seize the exact moment when her subject's inner self was visible through his or her face made every one of Mrs Terada's portraits a masterpiece.

Not only her husband, but her friends, and the people she came into contact with every day, were subjects for her camera, though there were more pictures of Mr Terada than there were of anyone else. Even Mr Kawakami of the camera shop was immortalized in one of her portraits, reflected in the glass of his store's front window as he bent over the counter, examining a customer's prints. It was an excellent likeness, and when Mr Kawakami first saw it, he begged Mrs Terada to let him have the negative, so that he could make an enlargement to hang in the store as an advertisement. But Mrs Terada had refused. The pictures she took were her own personal memories – not to be shared with others, except by special invitation.

Unlike so many photographers, Mrs Terada was not obsessive about showing her photos to other people. The sensitivity that made her such an excellent portrayer of faces extended to displaying her photographs. She could sense when her audience wanted to move on to another photo, and when they were absorbed in the postcard-sized representations of her past (she never had her photos enlarged). She always seemed able to tell when her audience was starting to become bored with the photos, and managed to close the album and return it to the shelf before ennui set in, almost always leaving her companion wanting to see more, and never leaving them feeling that they'd seen too many.

After her husband's death following a stroke, Mrs Terada's friends expected her to give up her photographic habit, but she seemed to have no intention of doing so. In fact, she caused a slight frisson among her friends by appearing at both the wake and the funeral with her camera clearly visible in her bag. Much to the relief of those attending, she didn't choose either of those occasions as the subject of her daily picture. In fact, looking at her album later, one of her friends worked out that the picture for the day of the wake was of a rose in full bloom, and that for the funeral was of a white heron in the stream behind her house.

Mr Terada had not been a wealthy man, but he had owned his own house, and, like most Japanese of his generation, had saved a considerable sum of money, so there was no need for his widow to consider moving. She obviously mourned his loss, but it was difficult for her friends to tell what she was really feeling. Certainly her appearance and her speech gave no indication of any deep grief.

A close-up shot of the smoke curling up from incense burning on a grave was one of the few reminders of Mr Terada after his death that she seemed to preserve in the albums, along with some pictures of his grave. Immediately after the funeral, for a while the photos became almost obsessively focused on flowers, typically with bright bold colours, and young children playing. Later they changed back to landscapes in more subdued tones, and a more general range of subjects, with more portraits of her friends. Like Mr Kawakami, the friends wanted copies of these pictures, but Mrs Terada refused all these requests, too. Her albums were her private memories, not to be given away to anyone, but only shared at her discretion.

About three years after her husband had died, Mrs Terada's friends noticed a change in her pictures.

"Isn't this rather a strange composition?" they would ask, puzzling over a photo that, although the subject was recognizable, seemed to lose the essence of itself that had been such a strong feature of her earlier photos.

"I'm experimenting," was Mrs Terada's reply on these occasions. "I feel I've reached my limit in the style I was using before, and it's time for me to start doing something new." It sounded like a reasonable enough answer, but there was a slight snap in her voice, hardly detectable, but still present, and the photo viewing session usually came to a swift halt after a visitor had expressed such an opinion. It wasn't that Mrs Terada was rude to her visitors, or even seemed anxious to lose their company, but they soon sensed that they were not welcome in the private world of her photo albums. The next time they visited, though, all seemed to be forgotten and forgiven, and they were invited to share Mrs Terada's memories with her once again.

It didn't stop her friends from talking among themselves. They'd always been somewhat proud, in a vicarious way, of Mrs Terada's talent, telling themselves that they were rubbing shoulders with an unknown and unrecognised reclusive genius of the photographic world. Now they were not so sure.

"Did you see the photograph she took last month?"

"Which one are you talking about?"

"That one of the temple over the road which was completely out of focus. You could tell what it was, of course, but it really didn't look like her kind of photo at all."

"Yes, I saw that. I was really surprised that she kept that one."

"Well, you know she takes only one photo every day, and there must be no gap in the series. I suppose she had to put it into the album if it was the only one she had."

"But it's not the only one like it."

"No, I noticed that. Quite a few of her photos are, well... if someone other than Mrs Terada had taken them, I would say they were rubbish, quite honestly. But since she knows what she's doing with that camera, I suppose it's not for me to judge. All I can say really is that it's not my kind of picture and I didn't like it."

"What did you say to her?"

"Nothing. You know how touchy she gets about that sort of thing these days."

And it was true. There was much more of a noticeable snap in Mrs Terada's voice when her photos were questioned, and the album shut quicker, almost with a bang.

It wasn't the only thing that her friends noticed. Mrs Suzuki, one of Mrs Terada's neighbours, saw her in the supermarket one day. Always being interested in her neighbours' doings (her husband called it 'being nosy', but she saw it as displaying her powers of observation and caring for others), Mrs Suzuki looked into the other's basket.

"Oh, you're buying chicken liver?" she asked. "I thought you didn't eat liver at all. Didn't you tell me once that you never ate liver?"

"I don't. Did I really pick up a pack of liver instead of minced chicken? How careless of me."

When relating the incident later to Mrs Horiuchi, Mrs Suzuki continued, "And then she went back to the refrigerator where they keep the chicken and just stood there for a few minutes, looking at things there. And then she started feeling all the packs of meat. Well, then the manager came out and watched her, and then he asked her what she wanted – I think – I was too far away to hear everything."

"And then?"

"She said something to him, and he picked up a pack of what looked like chicken mince and put it in her basket."

"Strange," said Mrs Horiuchi.

"Strange," agreed Mrs Suzuki.

Another time, Mrs Suzuki saw Mrs Terada coming out of the house wearing one black and one brown shoe.

"Did you know?" she asked, pointing to Mrs Terada's feet.

"Know what?" asked Mrs Terada in reply.

"You have a brown shoe on one foot and a black shoe on the other."

"Oh, how stupid of me," she said, turning round and going back into the house.

It was Mrs Horiuchi who got to the heart of it all. She had been invited to tea with Mrs Terada, and as always was invited to share memories of the past.

"And this was taken in the garden," said Mrs Terada, turning the page of an album that held pictures from ten years ago, and pointing to a picture of children playing on the beach.

Mrs Horiuchi looked at her. "Are you sure?"

"Of course I'm sure. I remember all my pictures and when I took them."

"But… but this is a picture of the beach."

Mrs Terada laughed. "Oh, how silly. Did I turn over two pages at once?" She flipped back a page, and there, in the same position on the page as the beach picture was the smiling face of Mr Terada in the back garden of their home.

Mrs Horiuchi looked at her hostess, but there seemed to be no real sign of embarrassment. She made the appropriate noises as Mrs Terada went through the other pictures in the album, but there were no more mistakes in identification.

"More tea?" asked Mrs Terada. "I'll just pop into the kitchen and make some more." She rose, taking the teapot with her.

Filled with an awful suspicion, Mrs Horiuchi got up, and as silently as she could manage, swiftly moved to the shelf holding the photo albums, and pulled out the current album, started two or three months earlier. She had never seen inside it, and neither, to the best of her knowledge, had any of her friends. She opened it, and gazed in horror at its contents.

Though the photographs were neatly and precisely arranged on the pages, the photographs themselves were no more than blurs. Some appeared to be completely black, and some were so over-exposed and light that it was impossible to tell what they were meant to represent. Almost all the others were out of focus, and, perhaps most shocking of all, some were arranged upside-down in the album.

Mrs Horiuchi quickly closed the book and returned it to its place before sitting down. Her mind raced through all the terrifying possibilities, but only one made sense, in the light of all the other strange things that had been happening.

Was she the one to talk to Mrs Terada and get her to face facts? Better her than that nosy busybody Mrs Suzuki. But where to begin?

"Can I help you?" she called through to the kitchen.

"No, thank you," came the reply. There was a silence followed by the sound of the hot water pot being used, and then a scream followed by a crash.

"What is it?" called Mrs Horiuchi, leaping to her feet as quickly as her arthritis would allow. She arrived in the kitchen to see Mrs Terada's face screwed up in pain, and the hot water pot lying on the floor in a pool of steaming hot water, beside the broken shards of the teapot.

"I've... scalded... my... hand," gasped out Mrs Terada. Quickly, Mrs Horiuchi turned on the cold faucet in the sink, and took Mrs Terada's hand, guiding it under the stream of cold water.

"Keep it there," she told Mrs Terada, using a tone of voice she hadn't employed since her children were in elementary school. "Do you have medicines in your bathroom?" Mrs Terada nodded, her face still screwed up. Mrs Horiuchi soon found the tube of ointment and returned to the kitchen. "This looks bad," she said, looking at the red hand, that already appeared to be swelling. "Now let's do something about it before we call the doctor. Sit down on this chair." As gently as she could, she took Mrs Terada's hand and dried it before spreading ointment over it. Mrs Terada winced with pain several times, despite all the care that Mrs Horiuchi took.

"What happened?" asked Mrs Horiuchi.

Mrs Terada seemed a little embarrassed. "My hand sort

of slipped," she explained. "I'm not really sure. I just found myself pouring water straight out of the pot over my hand."

"I really think you should go to hospital," said Mrs Horiuchi. "That really does look serious, and I think a doctor should look at it. You probably need to spend the night in the hospital. Don't worry about your house. I'll make sure that everything's locked up and safe, and my husband and I will keep an eye on it while you're away." She pulled out her mobile phone and explained the situation. "An ambulance will be here in about ten minutes, they say. Stay here in the kitchen. I know I can't find everything you need, but I can find most of your things, I think."

"Don't forget my camera," said Mrs Terada.

Mrs Horiuchi stopped dead in her tracks. "You won't need that. Really, you don't need it now, do you?" she said. Her voice was gentle.

Mrs Terada looked as though she was about to cry. "What do you mean?" she asked.

"You know very well what I mean." There was a long pause. "I wish you'd told me earlier. I could have helped you."

Mrs Terada sat in the chair, silent tears running down her face. "When did you find out? How long have you known? Does everyone know?"

"Only a few minutes ago. And as far as I know, I'm the only one. Though other people know there's something strange going on."

"I suppose it's high blood pressure or something like that. It's been going on for some time, but the last two months or so have been really bad. I can hardly see anything straight in front of me. Just to the sides, and then it's all blurred. I can manage most things, but not my camera any more. And then I do silly things like this."

"Why didn't you say something? Or go to a doctor?"

"It's so embarrassing. I don't know why I didn't say anything. Pride, I suppose. No-one likes to admit that they're getting older. But it's more than that. My camera is everything to me. It helps me remember the good times and the bad. I need to take those photographs, even when I can't see them properly any more. Just touching them helps me remember where I was and what I was doing that day."

The two sat in silence for a while.

"I'll pack your camera with your things," said Mrs Horiuchi after a while. "On one condition."

"What's that?"

"You tell the doctor all about your eyes. I am sure there is something they can do for you."

*L*ike all good tales, Mrs Terada's story has a happy ending. Her hand healed, even though she had scalded it quite seriously. More importantly, the hospital was able to make a precise diagnosis of her eye condition, and told her that simple surgery would restore most of her vision, at least for a few years. Mrs Terada was nervous about this, but after talking it over with Mrs Horiuchi, who visited her in the hospital every day, she decided to go ahead and have the operation. To her delight, she could see much better a few days after the surgery, and a new pair of glasses helped to bring her back to almost normal.

When she came out of hospital, she amazed Mr Kawakami at the camera shop.

"Show me one of those digital cameras," she demanded. "Just a small one, but one that will take good photos."

"Are you giving up your film camera?" he asked.

"No, not at all, but now I'm feeling greedy. I have my sight back for now, and I want to use it while I have it, so I'm going to take more pictures. I'll still take my daily picture with this," pointing to the old camera, "but I think there's so much to see around me, it would be a shame to waste any of it."

And, armed with her new eyes and her new digital camera, Mrs Terada went around taking her perfect pictures once again. To her delight, she was able to work out for herself how to hook up her camera and show her new digital photos on her large TV, allowing her to see them even when her eyes became tired.

Her friends, once they knew the story, rallied round and offered support and help, but Mrs Terada, with a touch of her old self, waved them away.

"But don't think I'm going to keep quiet when I need help in the future. I've learned my lesson about that," she told Mrs Suzuki over tea one afternoon. "And now," reaching for the TV remote, "let's just look at the photos of last week's softball game, shall we? But before that, can you just face into the light a little more?"

Click.

MRS SAKAMOTO'S GROUSE

"What's that?" Mrs Sakamoto asked Mr Hashiba, pointing to a bottle on the shelf behind the counter. "I don't think I've seen that before, have I?"

"It's whisky," replied the shopkeeper, "from Scotland. Just in. That's why you haven't seen it before."

Mrs Sakamoto pursed her lips. Mr Sakamoto, while he had been alive, had often talked of whisky. Indeed, he had probably drunk quite a lot of it in his time as a junior manager at his company, mainly in the form of heavily diluted *mizuwari*, topped off with Titanic-killing blocks of ice, but he had never brought any into the house, nor had Mrs Sakamoto ever encouraged him to do so. A little saké at New Year was her limit, and even after a few sips, she had to admit that she felt a bit giddy.

"No, what I really meant was, what's that picture on the label?" she asked. "It looks like a bird."

"It is a bird," replied Mr Hashiba. "It's a...," and he fetched the bottle down from the shelf to see more closely. "It says it's a 'grouse', I think," spelling out the English word and pronouncing it to rhyme with 'toes', and then correcting himself, making it rhyme with 'house'.

"Whatever that is," said Mrs Sakamoto, getting out her purse to pay for the vegetables and eggs that had just been rung up on the till.

"Whatever that is," agreed Mr Hashiba. He peered at the label again. "It also says that it's 'famous'," (again he used the English word).

"That means we should have heard of it, doesn't it?" said Mrs Sakamoto. "And we haven't. Does that make us stupid or something?"

"Just old," answered Mr Hashiba. "We're getting on, you and I."

There was no answer to that. At over eighty years old,

Mrs Sakamoto certainly didn't feel young. And Mr Hashiba wasn't that much younger, if truth be told. But the fact that there was a bird that she'd never heard of, and it was meant to be famous (for Mrs Sakamoto understood the meaning of the English word) worried her. Not that she expected to know everything that there was to know in this world, but it worried her. Of course she couldn't be expected to remember the names of the TV personalities and the singers and the politicians and the prime ministers and so on. All of these changed so often and they weren't important. But she had always felt that she had been interested in nature. She put out crumbs for the birds every morning, and spent a long time watching them, and spent several hours each week (at least when the weather was fine) walking in the woods and hills around the town.

She had remembered the spelling of the English word, and when she got home, she hauled the heavy English-Japanese dictionary off the shelf, and looked up the word. Well, it was there, after a little searching (she was sure that it had little to do with grumbling, though that was interesting). A *raichō*. Well, well. There was always something to learn. But famous?

The whisky was from Scotland, Mr Hashiba had said to her. That was in England, wasn't it? Another trip to the bookcase. But it all seemed too confusing. England seemed to be two or three countries, not just one, and Scotland seemed to be a separate country, but it was part of England as well. It didn't make an awful lot of sense. And none of it explained why the grouse was famous. It wasn't the national bird of Scotland or anything, as far as she could tell. In fact, there was no mention of a grouse anywhere in the description of Scotland, but it did seem like an interesting country for all that.

She started to wonder how many other things there were about Scotland that she didn't know about. Men wearing skirts? Well, that wasn't that different from Japan, where men wore kimono, she supposed, but she was glad that she didn't have to look at Japanese men's knees. And the history of Scotland seemed a bit like that of Japan, where the different families had quarrelled and warred against each other for a long time. And tartans! Mrs Sakamoto had owned a tartan rug for a long time, and she'd just thought of it as a pretty pattern. Now she realised that the colours and the size of the squares actually meant something to the right person. Unfortunately, her book only gave examples of a few tartans, and her rug wasn't one of them. Who would know about these things? She was going to have to do more research.

The next day saw her at the local public library, pulling out reference books in an attempt to find out more about these strange people living in their islands (she discovered that, just like Japan, there were lots of small islands where these people lived) and mountains. She got side-tracked by the description of porridge, which sounded rather nasty to her. But then as she told herself, it probably wasn't that unlike the okayu rice gruel she sometimes ate when she felt unwell. But the tartans were fascinating. Armed with the book she'd borrowed from the library, she bought herself a Buchanan tartan handkerchief. Quite a pretty tartan, she thought to herself. And Scotland certainly sounded like an interesting place. She thought again about the bird she'd seen on the bottle, the grouse. Perhaps they had one at the local zoo. It would do no harm if she were to go and check, anyway. Perhaps at the weekend.

The next Saturday, Mrs Sakamoto was standing in front of the enclosure where the solitary black grouse was caged. He (Mrs Sakamoto had checked the gender from the label on the cage) didn't seem terribly happy. He was rather a handsome bird, though, with his flashes of red around his head and his smart black plumage.

"What does he eat?" she asked one of the attendants who was passing.

"Mainly berries and things. But he's getting old, so he doesn't eat very much these days."

Mrs Sakamoto felt sorry for the grouse, who was pacing seemingly aimlessly in small circles around his food bowl. She'd seen from her reading that grouse lived on open moors and that kind of area, and it didn't seem right to keep him in a small cage like the one he was in. For some reason, he didn't seem to have a name, though some of the other animals had cute or appealing names. Not a happy bird, she decided. She turned away from the cage and prepared to go home. On the way out of the zoo gate, she turned into the souvenir shop. It was the meeting of her quilting group next Monday, and it was a tradition for everyone in turn to bring some sweets or biscuits. This week was Mrs Sakamoto's turn, and she decided to take along a snack that was a little different, like animal crackers or something along those lines.

She found what she wanted, and stood waiting to pay

when her eye was caught by a sign. "Adopt one of our animals," it said. Right there and then, Mrs Sakamoto's mind was made up. She was going to adopt the grouse, and she announced her intention to the girl behind the counter when she bought her biscuits.

"Just a moment," said the girl, and picked up the telephone by her till. "Would you mind waiting over there, please? Someone will be along to talk to you in a few minutes."

She waited and thought. Maybe adopting the grouse would be too expensive. Was it really something she wanted to do? She thought a little harder, but her mind was made up by the time an older man appeared to talk to her.

She explained how she was taken with the grouse, and felt sorry for him, and how she would like to adopt him. The zoo official listened sympathetically, and shook his head.

"Of course, we're very grateful to you for your offer. But he's hardly one of our most glamorous animals, is he? And quite frankly, we don't expect him to live much longer. We have some very charming baby monkeys, if you'd like to sponsor one of them."

"I think he needs a friend," said Mrs Sakamoto firmly. "Maybe he's not the most beautiful or cutest animal in your zoo, but I like him. And if he's going to die soon, then it's only right he should be looked after in his old age. How much does it cost to sponsor him for a year?"

The zoo official gave her a figure. "That's my best guess off the top of my head. It certainly wouldn't be more than that, and it would probably be a lot less."

In any case, it was much less than Mrs Sakamoto had imagined it might be. "Give me your bank details, and

I'll send you a year's sponsorship money tomorrow," she told the zoo official, who scratched his head, rather puzzled by this insistent old lady. "Or would you rather I gave you the money now?" She reached into her purse, and handed over the amount the official had just mentioned.

"I'll… I'll give you a receipt and take your details," he replied. "Please come with me to my office?" he invited. As he sat at his desk and wrote out the receipt, he looked up. "As the sponsor of this bird, you have the privilege of naming him. Please let us know when you've decided on a name, and we'll put it up on a plaque on his cage, along with your name."

"I know what his name is," said Mrs Sakamoto firmly. "His name is Donald." It was a name that had caught her eye when she was looking through the books on Scotland, and it seemed appropriate. "Don't bother about my name, though. That's really not very important."

"Can I ask … ?" asked the zoo official. He seemed puzzled. "Can I ask why you are so attached to this particular bird?"

It would have been silly to admit that she'd been attracted by the picture on the side of a whisky bottle, so Mrs Sakamoto gave some sort of half-hearted reply about just having seen Donald in his cage and feeling sorry for him.

"Well, I'm not going to criticise your choice," said the zoo official. "Everyone has their own favourite animals, and there's no accounting for what some people like. Why, we even have some people who like our naked mole rats. Certainly," he looked down at his notebook, "Donald is more attractive, to my eyes, at least, than they are."

Mrs Sakamoto thanked him and walked home.

She went to see Donald quite a lot after that – in fact, most weekends when the weather was good, and sometimes once or twice in the middle of the week as well. As a sponsor of one of the animals, she was allowed to enter the zoo without paying the admission charge, and the keepers and other zoo officials got to know her by sight as she sat on the bench in front of Donald's cage. After a while, they got to know her by name and always greeted her whenever they saw her. Sometimes they even allowed her to add her own little treats to Donald's feeding bowl. The nuts and fruit she brought along seemed to be appreciated, and it gave her a good feeling whenever Donald gobbled them up before his other food.

One day she arrived at the cage, but there was no Donald to be seen. She looked around her, and one of the young female keepers who looked after the birds noticed her standing by the enclosure, looking old and helpless.

"I'm very sorry, Mrs Sakamoto," the keeper told her. "But your Donald is not at all well. We found him lying on the floor of his cage yesterday evening, and we immediately took him into the zoo infirmary."

"What is it, do you know?" asked Mrs Sakamoto. For some reason, this illness of a bird seemed to be really important to her. She had to know more.

"I really don't know, but since I know you are his sponsor, and you are so fond of coming here, I am sure I can let you talk to the vet, if you'd like."

"Yes, if you would be so kind as to arrange that, please. I'd be most grateful."

"What is it?" she asked the vet some ten minutes later.

"Old age, I'm afraid," replied the vet. "Poor old thing."

"I'm so glad you feel sorry for him as well," said Mrs Sakamoto. "It does sound rather stupid, I suppose, but

I'd got rather fond of Donald. At least, I suppose so. I'd just sort of got used to coming here and seeing him." She suddenly realised that her eyes had absurdly filled with tears. She fished in her pocket for a handkerchief, and dabbed at her eyes. "Would there be any point in my seeing him now?"

The vet was a little taken aback by this, but he was a kindly man, both to his animal patients, and the humans with whom he had to deal. "Mrs Sakamoto, I have to tell you that he isn't in a good way at all."

"He's not dead, is he?"

The vet shook his head. "No, he's not, but he may go from us any day now. Quite frankly, I advise you to remember him as he was when you first saw him, and try not to get too upset if you can help it when he does die. He's had a good long life. These birds don't usually live more than a few years in the wild and the zoo has had your bird since he was a chick over eleven years ago. And I want you to know that he doesn't seem to be in any pain at all. I think that he really has just gone to sleep, and he'll never wake up. Just like some old people do."

Mrs Sakamoto shook her head as if to clear it. "Well, thank you very much. I do appreciate your taking the time to talk to a silly old woman."

"Not at all," the vet replied, flustered. "I mean, you're not silly at all. I am so glad that you took the time to appreciate one of our animals here so much."

*T*he next morning, Mrs Sakamoto received a call from the zoo. It confirmed that Donald had died in the night.

"The vet asked me to tell you specially that there was no pain. He just went to sleep and never woke up."

"Thank you. And the body?" asked Mrs Sakamoto.

"At this zoo, as I'm sure you have discovered, we treat our animals with dignity. In December there will be a memorial service at the local Buddhist temple for Donald and the other animals who have died in the year, and we will be sending you an invitation to attend, if you wish. Donald's body will be cremated with all due respect. Please do not worry about him."

"I understand," replied Mrs Sakamoto. "Thank you."

She put down the phone, collected her bag, and put on her coat before going out. Before she caught the train, she paid a call to Mr Hashiba's shop.

About an hour later, the zoo attendant who had been the bearer of the news about Donald's illness the previous day recognised Mrs Sakamoto, who was sitting in front of the empty cage. A paper cup was in her hand, and she appeared to be swaying a little. Dropping the mop and bucket she had been carrying, the attendant hurried towards the huddled figure.

"I'm so sorry," she said. "Are you all right?"

Mrs Sakamoto raised a tear-blurred face. "All right," she slurred. "Come and sit down beside me. Have a drink." She pulled a bottle out of her bag, followed by another paper cup. The attendant watched as Mrs Sakamoto sloshed a centimetre or two of amber liquid into the cup.

"Not too much for you," said Mrs Sakamoto, waving a warning finger. "You're on duty, aren't you? Never mind. Come on. Sit down."

The attendant looked around, and sat down, accepting the cup that Mrs Sakamoto was holding out towards her. "All right, but just for a moment."

"To Donald," said Mrs Sakamoto, holding out her own cup towards the cage.

"To Donald," the attendant replied. She sipped and coughed. "That's good, but it is a bit strong, isn't it?"

"But it warms you up, and helps you forget things." A pause. "Do you think Donald had a happy life?"

The other drank and considered. "Not bad, I suppose."

"Your cup's empty, dear. Let me pour a little more. I was very fond of coming here and watching him, you know. Do you think he recognised me?"

"I don't really think—" She changed her original sentence in mid-flow, as she looked at Mrs Sakamoto's face, and realised that there could only be one answer to the question. "I don't really think that anyone could doubt that. You were so good to him, and visited him so often. How could he not recognise you?"

Mrs Sakamoto smiled. "That's what I thought," she said weakly. "Some more?" holding out the bottle. "Just a splash," as a couple of centimetres went into the cup.

"I shouldn't, but thank you."

About thirty minutes later, one of the senior keepers came by. He recognised both women sitting on the bench in the warm spring sun, propped up against each other, seemingly fast asleep. "Poor old bat," he said to himself, as he noticed the half-empty bottle and empty cup beside Mrs Sakamoto. "Who would have guessed she'd take it so hard? But," shaking his head, as he noticed the second cup beside the other figure, "Adachi-san shouldn't have been drinking with her. She should have stopped her. But what on earth have they been drinking at this hour of the morning, anyway, to send them off like that? He picked up the bottle, and a slow smile spread over his face as he saw the picture on the label, and spelled out the English words, "The Famous Grouse".

THE OLD HOUSE

*T*he house at the end of the lane stood empty and forbidding, as it had done for the past five years. Taro Okamura and his best friend Masaaki used the garden as their private hiding place when they needed to discuss private things. Things that weren't for parents' ears. Or for sisters' ears, either. Taro suffered from a surfeit of older sisters – four, to be precise, and he sometimes envied Masaaki, who had only two.

As the "baby boys" of their families, the two were mothered to the point of suffocation and while Taro often enjoyed the attention, there were limits to what he could put up with. Nine years old was almost grown up, for heaven's sake.

Masaaki felt the same, even though he was only eight, half a year younger than Taro, and so the two of them regularly escaped together to the sanctuary of Mr Koizumi's garden.

They called it that, even though Mr Koizumi had died five years ago and they'd never known him. He hadn't been liked in the neighbourhood. His house was easily the largest in the district, and the garden had originally been a thing of wonder, according to Taro's parents who'd seen it once. But only once, because Mr Koizumi had been a reclusive money-lender, asking large sums for his services, and even reportedly driving some of his creditors to suicide as the result of his insistent demands for repayment.

Even though he'd owned the largest house and the best garden in the district, he'd never offered its use to the neighbourhood group for use in the summer festivals. Instead, the *mikoshi*, the portable shrine, was carried around the district, and had to stand for the priest's blessing in the premises of the local Daihatsu dealer, where the gaudy gilded decorations contrasted sadly with the grimy oily forecourt.

All this rankled. When Mr Koizumi had died, there had been a lot of interest in the property – it was, after all, one of the best sites in the neighbourhood for a building – and there had been rumours that a builder from Tokyo was going to buy the land, level the small hill that formed part of the property, and build a block of hideous new apartments on the site.

Whatever the feelings of the local community had been towards Mr Koizumi, they certainly weren't well-disposed towards Tokyo developers. A signboard was put up announcing the planned construction, meetings of out-raged residents were held, and miraculously, the development was stopped. There were some protests from the developers, who complained that the halt to the building was an infringement of their rights, but this was shouted down by the community, who argued that the local water supply, roads, schools, and so on, were inadequate to cope with the increased population that would move into the area if the apartment building went ahead.

And so Mr Koizumi's garden stood empty and deserted – a perfect place for Taro and Masaaki to escape from their womenfolk, and for them to act out their dreams. Taro was the more realistic in his ambitions. His fantasies typically revolved around what he had seen on the television news that night. For example, the previous week there had been a lot of reporting on anti-whaling activists. Taro had immediately suggested that he become a whaling ship, and Masaaki should become a whale. Masaaki reluctantly agreed, on condition that the roles be reversed after a while. Bamboo canes, plucked from the garden, and tipped with old tennis balls (collected from the woodland behind the tennis club) made harpoons, and taking turns to become whaler and whale, the boys developed sophisticated techniques for flinging and avoiding harpoons.

Today Taro announced that they were going to play "Elections".

"I stand on this log here and speak to you and tell you things," he explained.

"And what do I do?" asked Masaaki.

"You applaud what I say, of course. You clap and cheer."

"What if I don't like what you're saying?"

"You will. People always like what these politions – politickers – whatever they're called – say."

"All right," grumbled Masaaki, and moved to take his place as the electorate.

Taro climbed onto his log, and started his speech. His ideas of what politicians actually said were rather vague, but he had an excellent ear, and the overall effect was very similar to that of a political speech. In the middle of a rant about taxes (he was in favour of raising them, for reasons unclear to his audience, or indeed, to him), he stopped short.

"What was that?" he asked, looking over Masaaki's shoulder and pointing.

"How should I know?" asked Masaaki, a little cross and bored. "I don't have eyes in the back of my head. What are you talking about, anyway?"

"There was a face in the window of the house." Taro's voice shook a little. "I swear it."

Masaaki turned round. "Which window?"

"That one by the front door." Taro pointed it out.

Masaaki got up from where he had been sitting, and moved towards Taro. He clambered onto the log beside his friend and looked. "You saw your reflection," he declared. "See?" He waved his hand. "See?" he repeated. "My reflection's waving back to us. Silly."

Taro considered this, but only for half a second. "It's you who's silly," he retorted. "I don't have a long white beard like that face did."

"You never said that."

"Yes I did."

"Didn't."

"Did."

"Didn't."

"Did so."

"Did n—" Masaaki broke off. "Look! There's your face again. And it has a beard, just like you said."

Both boys looked at the wide staring eyes, framed in a tangle of bushy white hair, with a long straggly beard hanging from the chin. As they watched, a thin bony hand appeared in the window, beckoning them to draw near. They looked at each other.

"I'm going to see who it is," Masaaki said boldly.

"You mustn't," Taro told him. "I promised your mother I'd take care of you because you're only little."

"I'm not little. I'm nearly nine," Masaaki objected. "Anyway, I'm not scared, even if you are."

"I'm not scared," said Taro, but his face and the tone of his voice gave the lie to his words, "but it's probably one of those homeless people who attack you. I saw something on the television about them last week."

"That's rubbish," replied Masaaki. He started to move towards the house.

"Hey, wait for me!" shouted Taro, all pretence of bravery now forgotten, as Masaaki neared the house. Masaaki stopped. The face had gone from the window, but neither boy had noticed it disappear.

"Uh?" both boys exclaimed together.

"Still want to go and see?" asked Taro.

"Of course. Why not?" Masaaki tiptoed towards the window, and cupped his hands to peer through the dusty glass into the room inside.

Taro hung back. "Nothing?" he called, almost hopefully.

"Can't see anything. I'm going inside."

"Don't be stupid. How can you get in?"

"The window's open, I think." Masaaki was forcing open the frame as he spoke. It creaked as it slid open. "Oh!" A little cry as he clambered up over the sill and swung one leg inside the room.

"What?"

"Nothing. Just a big spider. Startled me."

"I hate spiders," Taro said firmly.

"Scaredy-cat."

"I am not. I just don't like them, that's all. And I'm not coming in if the place is full of them."

By now, Masaaki had dropped down inside the room and Taro lost sight of him. Taro was a little worried. It wasn't just the spiders. There was something creepy about the house, it seemed to him. "See anything?" he called. There was no answer. As he drew in his breath to shout to Masaaki again, the face reappeared at the half-open window. He could see it more clearly now. The straggly beard was in full view, and the dark piercing eyes seemed to be staring straight at him. Surely Masaaki was in the same room as this monster? Again the hand beckoned him closer. Despite his fear, his legs carried him closer to the window, against his better judgment – indeed, against his will.

He could see the face more clearly now. Grimy and wrinkled, it looked to Taro like the faces of some homeless people he'd seen in a park once when he'd been to Tokyo. If Masaaki was in danger from the man, it was up to him to save him. Right? Right. Taro wasn't the bravest of boys – he'd somehow managed to be away from school the day they tried out for catcher in the baseball team, and he had a knack for staying away from situations which looked as though they might end up in a fight. He decided that this was one of the times when he needed grown-ups – it wasn't going to be something he could solve easily on his own.

"Don't worry, Masaaki!" he called through the open window. "I'm going to get help." And he turned and fled back to his home.

It took a minute or so to persuade his mother, who'd just come back from shopping, to put on her shoes again and come to Koizumi's house to save Masaaki from whatever was happening to him. She nagged him all the time they were running down the lane.

How he should never, ever, go in there. And how wicked he was to persuade Masaaki to go with him. Taro was glad that it had been a politician day, and not a whaling day. She would probably have thrown a fit if she had heard about the harpoons.

"Which room?" she asked as they made their way through the bushes.

Taro pointed to the open window.

"I can't climb through that. Not in this skirt," she complained to him.

Take it off, then, Taro thought but didn't say. Women could be so impractical sometimes.

"Let's try the door," she said. Taro was sure the door

would be locked, but to his amazement, when his mother turned the handle and pulled, the door swung open.

"What on earth made Masaaki come in here?" asked his mother, holding a handkerchief over her nose. "It's so dusty and dirty."

"Masaaki!" called Taro.

There was an answering hail from the room where Masaaki had gone through the window, and in a few seconds, Masaaki himself appeared. "Is it really you, Taro? And Mrs Okamura? I'm so glad you're here." His face was pale.

"You wicked, naughty boy! What is your mother going to say?" Taro's mother gave vent to her frustration by smacking the dust off Masaaki's clothes as roughly as she dared. "Where were you?"

Masaaki led the way to the room where he had been waiting to be "rescued".

"Here. Just here." He pointed to a spot on the tatami matting next to the low table. There were two rather handsome teacups standing on it.

Taro's mother reached out to one of the cups and started to look at the bottom. It was a minor obsession of hers, finding out where pottery had been made. But before she had turned it over, she stopped suddenly.

"There's something in this. And it's still warm!" she exclaimed.

"Of course it's still warm," replied Masaaki in the voice he reserved for particularly stupid grown-ups.

"But how could you make tea?" asked Mrs Okamura. "There's no gas or water, is there?"

"I didn't make it. He did," replied Masaaki, obviously somewhat frustrated by the density of anyone over twelve years old. "The old man," he added.

"You mean there is someone else here?" asked Taro's mother. She seemed nervous about the idea.

"Oh, he's gone now," said Masaaki.

"Masaaki Kimura, you should be ashamed of telling stories like that." She recovered a little of her composure. "Of course there's no one here. I can see that for myself."

"I didn't mean in this room," he insisted. "I meant in this house. He went out of the house a few minutes before you arrived."

"And just where did he go?" asked Mrs Okamura. She had meant it to be a rhetorical question, but Masaaki had an answer.

"Back to hell, he said."

Taro looked at his friend, and his hair started to stand on end. Truth to tell, he was a little jealous. He was the one who invented things. That was his job, not Masaaki's. What was Masaaki talking about?

His mother was obviously annoyed. "Don't be so silly, Masaaki," she said. "Where is he?" She put down the teacup. "He can't be far away. This tea is still warm."

"We didn't pass anyone coming along the lane towards us, Mum," Taro pointed out.

"Well, maybe he's in the woods or something," she replied. "You said he was one of those homeless people."

"I said he looked like one of those homeless people," Taro corrected her.

"Well, you'd better show us to the kitchen and make sure you turned everything off," she told Masaaki. She had obviously decided that the idea of the old man was an invention of the boys, conveniently ignoring the evidence of the two cups on the table.

"I didn't make the tea, I told you," said Masaaki. "I don't know where the kitchen in this house is."

"Suit yourself," said Mrs Okamura. "Come with me," as she stalked out of the room.

"What really happened, Masaaki?" asked Taro. "Quick, while she's not listening."

"I came in, and he was sitting just there," pointing to the other side of the table from where he was standing, "with those two cups of tea. He asked me to sit down there," indicating a point on the floor by the table.

"And then?"

"And then he told me he was a spirit." Taro felt a chill run down his back. "He is dead, and in hell. And that on the day that he died – I mean, the day of the year when he died – if anyone comes into the house or the garden, he has to leave hell for a while because he has to be their host and offer them tea. Because he was so mean in his life, he said. Today's the day and so he came into the house as we came into the garden. He just was just sitting there with those dark eyes, watching me drink my tea."

"What did you talk about?"

"I didn't say anything, and he didn't either. He was a bit scary. Actually he was *really* scary. I didn't want to talk to him at all. Look." He pointed to where he had told the others he had been sitting. The dust on the tatami mats had been disturbed, and the tatami showed golden brown through the places where the gray coating of dust had been disturbed.

"Yes?"

"Now look at where he was sitting." The layer of dust on the other side of the table was smooth and even. "I think he was a demon – really evil – not just a spirit." He shivered.

"Come on, you two. What are you doing?" came Taro's

mother's voice. "I'm in the kitchen at the back of the house."

The two boys went through the empty dusty passages and found the kitchen, dark, and covered with cobwebs.

Mrs Okamura was standing by the kitchen sink. "Well, this hasn't been used for years. Where did the water come from?" The sink contained three scratchy dead leaves and a dead spider. She turned the tap. There was no water. She went to the gas cooker, which was likewise covered in dust. There were no pots or pans or kettles in sight. "This hasn't been used for years, either." She scratched her head. "I don't know what you've been up to, Masaaki, but you're not to do it again."

"Don't worry, Mrs Okamura, I won't," he replied.

And he was as good as his word. The next time Taro suggested playing in the garden, Masaaki refused to go there. In fact, they never played in the garden again that summer. And the next year the bulldozers came along and the block of apartments got built after all.

IF YOU ENJOYED THIS BOOK…

*T*hank you for reading these stories – I hope you enjoyed them.

It would be highly appreciated if you left a review or rating online somewhere.

You may also enjoy some of my other books, which are available from the usual outlets.

ALSO BY HUGH ASHTON

SHERLOCK HOLMES TITLES
Tales from the Deed Box of John H. Watson M.D.
More from the Deed Box of John H. Watson M.D.
Secrets from the Deed Box of John H. Watson MD
The Darlington Substitution
The Case of the Trepoff Murder
Notes from the Dispatch-Box of John H. Watson M.D.
Further Notes from the Dispatch-Box of John H. Watson M.D.
The Lichfield Murder
The Death of Cardinal Tosca
Without My Boswell
1894
Some Singular Cases of Mr. Sherlock Holmes
The Adventure of Vanaprastha

GENERAL TITLES

The Untime
The Untime Revisited
The Untime & The Untime Revisited
Balance of Powers
Leo's Luck
Beneath Gray Skies
Red Wheels Turning
At the Sharpe End
Angels Unawares
The Persian Dagger (with M. Lowe)

TITLES FOR CHILDREN (WITH ANDY BOERGER)

Sherlock Ferret and the Missing Necklace
Sherlock Ferret and the Multiplying Masterpieces
Sherlock Ferret and the Poisoned Pond
Sherlock Ferret and the Phantom Photographer
The Adventures of Sherlock Ferret

ABOUT THE AUTHOR

Hugh Ashton was born in the United Kingdom, and moved to Japan in 1988, where he lived until a return to the UK in 2016.

He is best known for his Sherlock Holmes stories, which have been hailed as some of the most authentic pastiches on the market, and have received favourable reviews from Sherlockians and non-Sherlockians alike.

He currently lives in the cathedral city of Lichfield with his wife, Yoshiko.

More about Hugh Ashton and some of his books may be found at HughAshtonBooks.com

www.ingramcontent.com/pod-product-compliance
Lightning Source LLC
Chambersburg PA
CBHW032051180726
48284CB00004B/1283

* 9 7 8 1 9 1 2 6 0 5 5 3 8 *